In memory of Auntie Kat whose bright shining light touched the hearts of everyone she met.

Thanks to Grandma, Auntie Charlotte
and our dear friends Naush and Sarah for all their help.

EVERYONE CAN SHINE
Author Hannah Barrios
Illustrator Helen Barrios
www.helenbarriosbooks.com

Everyone can SHINE

Author HANNAH BARRIOS
Illustrator HELEN BARRIOS

"I wish...
it wasn't like this."
Autumn thought, dragging her feet,
as she made her way along the high street.
"I wish I could make others smile again, like I used to!"
Autumn could see all the other small monsters
having fun and enjoying themselves.

DEEP, DEEP down inside, she often felt left out. Sometimes, without really thinking, she would say things. Things that were not very helpful.

Sometimes, without meaning to, her sadness made others sad too.

Suddenly, a small, spotty someone raced past Autumn.

"Don't

SMILE

too much or your face might hurt!"

Autumn shouted loudly.

The small, spotty someone stopped, turned and stared at the young monster.

Scared, Autumn ran away
and disappeared down a
narrow alleyway. She found
a tight corner, where she curled up
into a small ball and began to cry.

“Why’d you say that to me?” questioned the small, spotty someone, unexpectedly poking its head out from behind a wheelie bin.

Autumn looked up curiously, “I didn’t want to!” she muttered.

“Then why’d ya say it?
By the way: my name’s Sprocket...

Sprocket the Rocket...

faster than light and
quicker than sight!”

Sprocket darted out from his hiding place and looked thoughtfully at Autumn.

“You look sad!
I wonder...
are you a good person who is just hiding your kindness?”

Autumn looked surprised.
“That’s funny,” she said,
“because not so long ago,
I was a happy monster.
I made everyone smile…
but then the names started.”

“The names, what do you mean?” Sprocket asked.
“For them it was just a joke, but it didn’t feel like a joke to me. I could see right through them, and it WASN’T a joke!”

The two little monsters looked at one another sadly.

"You see," said Autumn nervously,
"I used to have this special ability... my tummy
would change colour depending on how I felt."

"Wow, that's sooooo coooool!"
Sprocket exclaimed.

"Now I'm just grey...
I've lost all my shine,"
continued Autumn.

"No-one can lose their shine,
they only put it away for a while,"
said Sprocket kindly.

"Don't hide

your true colours...

I bet they're AMAZING! I'd really like to see them!"

Autumn panicked. "Maybe another day. Got to go now," she called, running out of the alley.

After the sun had risen and set a few times,
and Autumn and Sprocket had played together,
they soon became good friends.

Some days later, Autumn was strolling through the park,
when suddenly she spotted Sprocket curled up,
shivering under a large weeping willow tree.

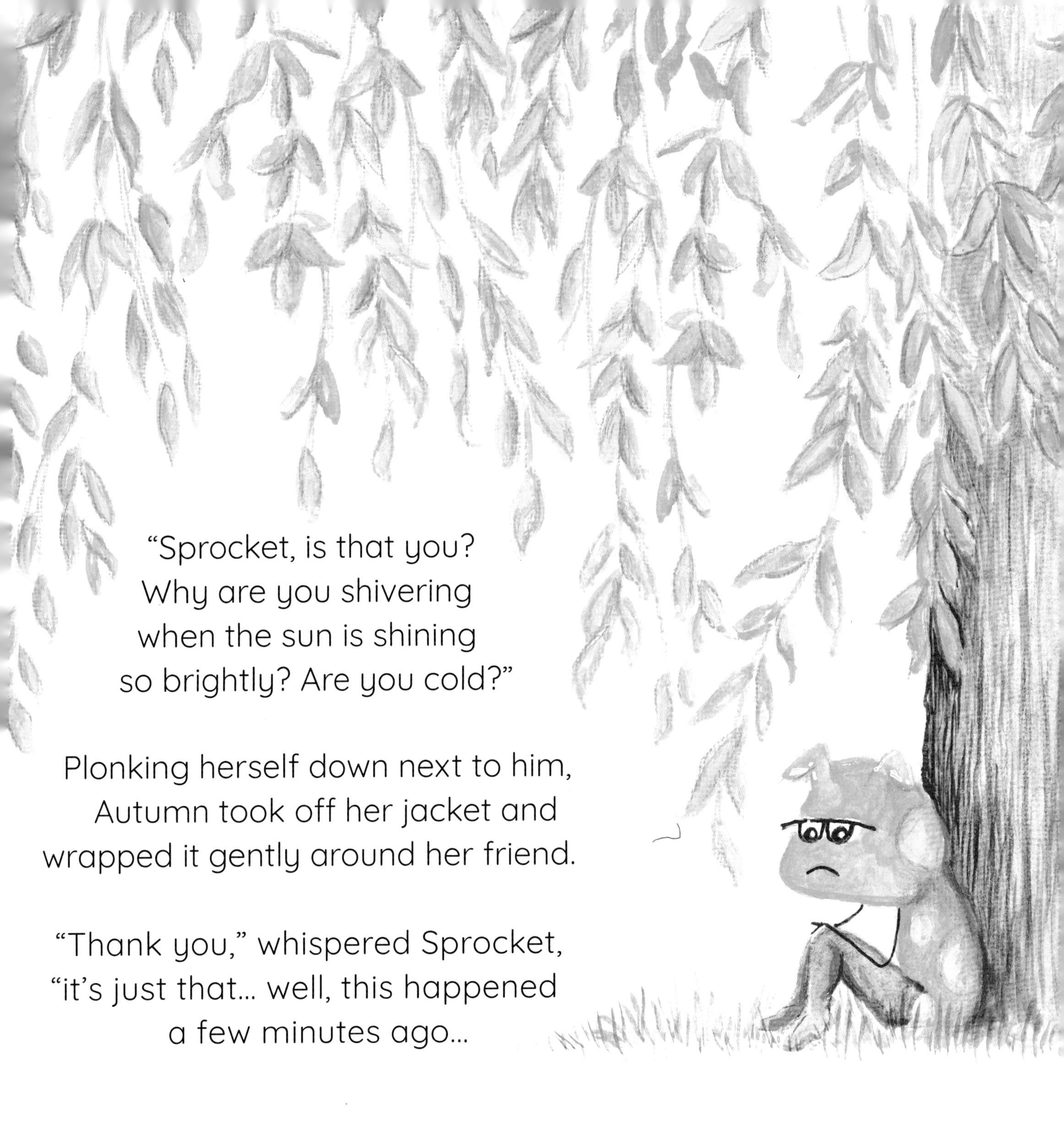

“Sprocket, is that you?
Why are you shivering
when the sun is shining
so brightly? Are you cold?”

Plonking herself down next to him,
Autumn took off her jacket and
wrapped it gently around her friend.

“Thank you,” whispered Sprocket,
“it’s just that… well, this happened
a few minutes ago…

the others started calling me names too."

Look who's friends with GRUMPY-PANTS!

Turtle face!

Spotty Botty and Smelly Belly f-r-i-e-n-d-s!

Green Alien and Cry Baby Chameleon!

Look who's hanging out with MISS MOODY MUPPET!

Realising that Sprocket was sad,
Autumn suddenly grasped her legs and curled up into a ball. Autumn was desperate to cover up her tummy, which was now turning a deep blue colour!

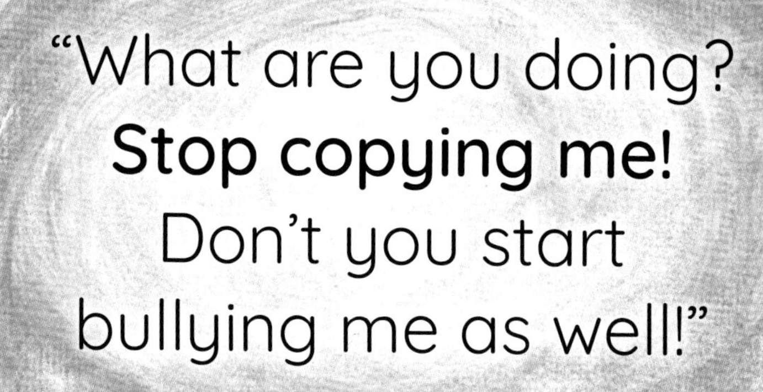

Sprocket shouted angrily.

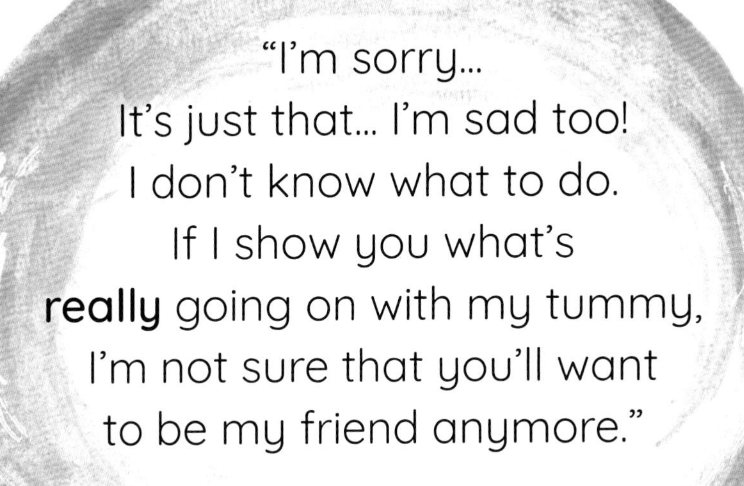

They sat looking at each other.
Both were a little sad...
both a little unsure.

“We’re friends aren’t we, you just need to trust me.”
Sprocket whispered reassuringly.

Slowly, Autumn uncurled herself revealing her tummy
and waited for her friend’s reaction.

"That's awesome...
that's so cool!

I've never had a friend who
understands exactly how I feel."

Sprocket giggled.

"My tummy started turning blue when I realised you were sad and then I felt sad as well," explained Autumn.
"Does it make you you feel scared when my tummy turns blue? Does it make you want to run away?" she asked.

“No, why should it?
Everyone can feel different things,
at different times and that’s OK.

If you don’t tell anyone how you feel,
how can they begin to understand you?

True friendship goes beyond feelings and what others might say.”

Sprocket jumped to his feet, “Come on, let’s go!”
Autumn leapt up and chased after her friend.
“Can I have a piggyback, pleeeease?” begged Sprocket.

“Come on then, let’s go!”

Autumn replied joyfully.

Autumn was SO happy that now she had someone who understood her. Can you guess what happened next?

She started to shine once again.
And she shone... **and she shone... and**

Autumn knew that as long as she kept shining, she would light up the lives of everyone she met.

"I knew you had it in you.
You just needed to
let it out !"

Smiling confidently, Autumn was no longer afraid
to show her true colours and to be herself.
As for those who made fun of her, Autumn decided
that although their words may still hurt, they could laugh
and they could snigger all they liked, but they would...

NEVER
stop her
shining
again!

Being yourself makes
you shine.
Being yourself makes
others shine
too!

YOU CAN SHINE BY....

Being a GOOD FRIEND.

Being KIND to yourself and to others.

HELPING OTHERS and ASKING FOR HELP.

REMEMBER... WORKING TOGETHER,

we can all find our TRUE COLOURS.

YOU ARE AN
AMAZING
star

I can SHINE

Author : Hannah Barrios

Hannah is an inspiring young writer, whose passion to bring joy to others motivates her work.

Through her stories, Hannah aims to encourage, empower and educate her readers. She hopes to inspire others to be their very best, finding strength to overcome adversities and discover their unique ability to shine.

Hannah is mixed race and has grown up respecting and celebrating both her Latin American and British heritage. She is a fun-loving, caring and creative individual, who loves swimming, musical theatre and art.

Illustrator : Helen Barrios

Helen's love of storytelling has taken her to many fascinating places. She has lived in Argentina, spent time with a nomadic tribe in Paraguay, hiked through the depths of the Bolivian jungle and listened to stories on the bustling streets of Thailand.

As a designer and illustrator, Helen loves collaborating with other authors, using her creativity to bring their ideas to life, whilst also producing her own books.

Helen lives in London, England with her Argentinian husband and their three children. Together they enjoy outdoor pursuits, international food and of course, exploring.

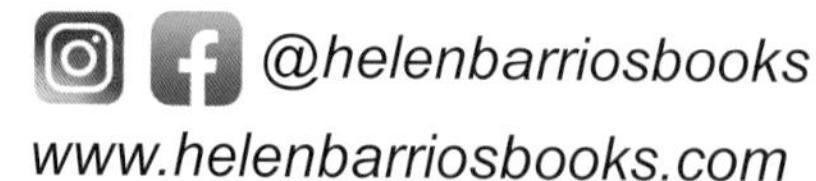

www.helenbarriosbooks.com